For my friend Bob,
who helped me walk
through the woods.
J.C.

For Ruby & Louis.
L.J.

JANETTA OTTER-BARRY BOOKS

A Walk in the Wild Woods copyright © Frances Lincoln Limited 2010
Text copyright © Lis Jones 2010
Illustrations copyright © Jim Coplestone 2010

First published in Great Britain and in the USA in 2010 by
Frances Lincoln Children's Books, 4 Torriano Mews,
Torriano Avenue, London NW5 2RZ

www.franceslincoln.com

British Library Cataloguing in Publication Data available on request

ISBN: 978-1-84507-956-7

Illustrated with watercolour

Printed in Dongguan, Guangdong, China by Toppan Leefung in January 2010

1 3 5 7 9 8 6 4 2

A Walk in the Wild Woods

Story by Lis Jones

Illustrations by Jim Coplestone

F

FRANCES LINCOLN
CHILDREN'S BOOKS

When Ruby and Rabby are together,
they aren't scared of many things,
but they are not too sure about going
for a walk in the wild woods.

"I'm a bit scared we might see a fox, Daddy," says Ruby.

"Don't worry, Ruby, you're safe with me," says Daddy.

Daddy and Ruby and Rabby walk past
the rustling trees towards the gate to the woods.
Suddenly there is a flash of orange
in the green grass, and Daddy calls,
"Look, Ruby, there's Foxy! He's chasing rabbits."

"Why is he doing that?" asks Ruby.
"Foxes can't go to the shops like we can, so they
have to catch rabbits to eat," says Daddy gently.

"That's bad for the rabbits, isn't it?"
says Ruby quietly.
"Yes, Ruby. But it will be good
for Foxy and his cubs to have
some dinner," says Daddy.

"Will Foxy eat me, Daddy?" asks Ruby.
"No, you're too big and strong. He only likes soft little rabbits," says Daddy.
"Sshh! You're scaring Rabby!" says Ruby.
"Oh yes! Sorry, Rabby," says Daddy.

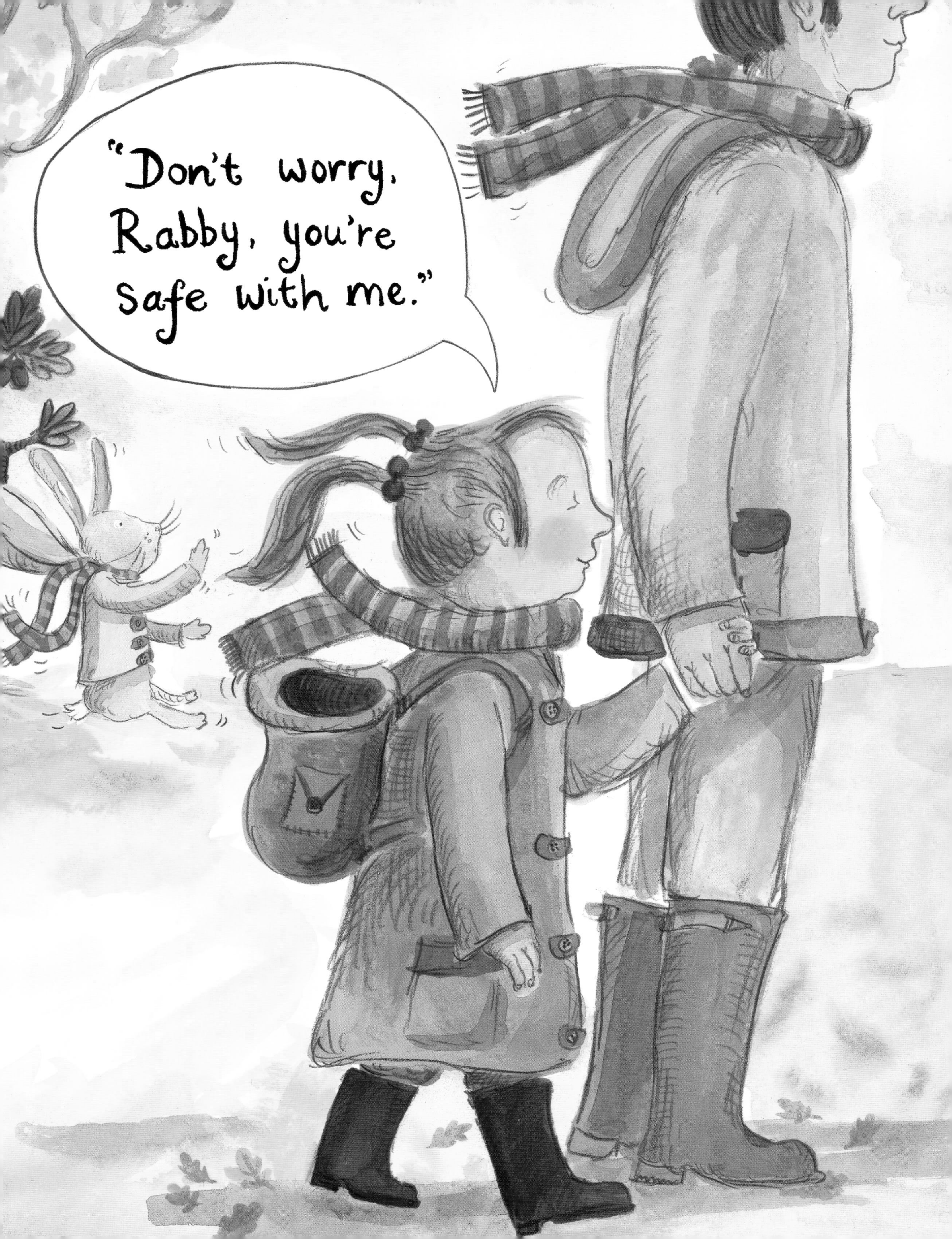
"Don't worry, Rabby, you're safe with me."

"Can Foxy hear us?" asks Ruby.

"Oh yes, Foxy can even hear an acorn drop," laughs Daddy.

"How about if we stay really quiet, Daddy?" whispers Ruby.
"Would Foxy know we're here?"

"Oh yes," Daddy whispers back.
"He'd be able to smell us."

"How does Foxy see at night?"
asks Ruby.

"Foxy has special eyes that can see in the dark," says Daddy.

"Rabby! How did you get here?" cries Ruby.
"I must have left you behind. How sad,
   you missed our lovely walk."

"We saw Foxy, didn't we, Ruby?" says Daddy.

"Yes, I know all about him now," says Ruby happily,

"and I'm not scared any more."